All Alone
at Christmas

For Zara
J.S.
For Tiggy – our trusted dog,
who's not scared of anything (except mice)
P.H.

ORCHARD BOOKS
338 Euston Road, London NW1 3BH
Orchard Books Australia
Level 17/207 Kent Street, Sydney, NSW 2000

First published in 2009 by Orchard Books.

Text © Justine Smith 2009
Illustrations © Paul Howard 2009

A CIP catalogue record for this book is available
from the British Library.

ISBN 978 1 40830 763 2

1 3 5 7 9 10 8 6 4 2

Printed in Great Britain

Orchard Books is a division of Hachette Children's Books,
an Hachette UK company.

www.hachette.co.uk

All Alone
at Christmas

Justine Smith

ORCHARD BOOKS

Chapter One

"Enough! Enough, Milo. I'm awake now!"
With a sleepy yawn and a chuckle, Katie
gently pushed the wriggly puppy off
her pillow. It was less than a week till
Christmas and as Katie looked across
her bedroom, she felt very excited. She
slept right at the top of the house, under
the eaves. Her bed, draped in floaty
curtains, took up almost the whole room.

Through a little oval window in the steeply sloped ceiling, Katie could see a dome of sky and the zigzag tips of the rooftops opposite. It was like sleeping up in the clouds, and she loved it.

Now Milo's soft brown eyes gazed at her. He licked her face again and gave her a doggy grin. His little tail wagged so frantically that his whole body wiggled.

"That was a lovely good-morning kiss, Milo!" Katie pulled him close for a cuddle. But the little puppy had other ideas – he squirmed loose and set off down the bed.

Katie sat up to watch him.

Still on the bed, Milo spotted Katie's feet poking up in a mound under the covers. He threw himself down on his side, wrapped his big paws around her toes, and gave them a nip.

"Ouch, Milo!" protested Katie, drawing her knees up. Milo got back up, and continued his wobbly progress towards the end of the bed. He gave her a quick backwards look, as if to check that she was still watching him.

What was he up to? Katie hugged her knees, rested her chin on them, and fixed her grey eyes steadily on her puppy, waiting to see what he would do next.

Milo's nose could smell something interesting. He rummaged about at the end of the bed and sat back unsteadily on his bottom. He was wearing one of Katie's bed socks on his head, draped demurely over one ear, and looking very pleased with himself. And he was nibbling thoughtfully on the *other* bed sock.

When are we getting up...? he seemed
to say. And: *What's for breakfast?*

"No, Milo – you silly thing," said Katie
tenderly, gently tugging the soggy sock
out of his mouth. But she took the hint.
With one swift movement she threw back
the covers, retrieved her wriggly puppy
from under them, and slid out of bed.

Downstairs, the kitchen table was covered in Christmas cards and envelopes. Katie's mum was writing very-last-minute Christmas cards, and looking harassed. "Um, Matt, can you remember what the Batleys called the new baby?" she said. "Oh no, I don't think I have their address anymore... Did they send us a card last year? Oh dear..."

Katie's dad slurped his tea and tried to help. "No, sorry, Kath, I did get out last year's list, but I think Milo ate it." He raised one eyebrow at Katie.

She clutched Milo closer. "Dad! He's only little, it's not his fault!"

And then Katie remembered that today was the day they were getting their Christmas tree, and she quickly forgot all about breakfast. "Can we go, can we go?"

she asked excitedly.

"Hmm…" said Dad, slowly. "I suppose if we went this early we'd be the first ones there."

"Oh please, Dad! Go on!" Katie hopped up and down, making Milo's ears flap, and her Dad laugh.

"Well, all right then, but we really can't take Milo – I need you to help me get the tree into the car."

For once Katie didn't argue. Milo was adorable at all times, of course, but he was also like a tiny tornado when they took him out in the car. He refused to sit still, and clambered over their laps, crossing from one side of the back seat to the other, poking his nose out of the little gap at the top of the window to discover what he could smell. He barked enthusiastically at everything and everyone as they went along, and howled happily if they played any music. Katie had to agree – it might not be a terribly good idea to take Milo with them!

"Milo, you stay at home with Mum," she told the crestfallen puppy. "Don't

11

worry, we'll get you the biggest, best tree there."

This was Milo's first Christmas and Katie wanted it to be perfect. The little puppy had a proper stocking, and he even had his own Christmas hat to wear on Christmas day. Katie had spent ages at the pet shop, choosing his present. She had already wrapped it – in the most crinkly paper she could find – and she knew Milo would love the paper as much as the present. And she couldn't wait for the Christmas tree to go up so she could put his parcel under it...

☆ ★ ★ ✳

Katie had always wanted a puppy. But, at first, Mum and Dad had bought her a hamster instead. Millie was a lovely, fluffy little thing, and Katie had tried to love her. She fed her every day, and cleaned out her cage all by herself, just to show Mum that she *could* be responsible for an animal. But Millie only cared about sunflower seeds and spinning in her wheel. And even though Katie picked her up and brushed her, she was a little...dull. And she did bite. Katie was very fond of her, but Millie was not the special friend she had longed for.

Eventually Katie had given up pestering Mum and Dad for a dog, but she never gave up hope. On every birthday, she would blow out the candles on her cake, squeeze her eyes tight and make the same wish. Every Christmas, her letter to Santa began the same way: *Dear Santa, please may I have a puppy...*

And then, just a few weeks ago, her luck had changed. Katie was in the living room, doing her homework. Grandma was in the kitchen, chatting to Dad about the exciting news – her neighbour's Labrador had a new litter of puppies! Katie's mum was there too, making an apple crumble. And suddenly, coming from the kitchen, Katie half-heard Grandma's voice:

"Actually, Matthew, there is one last puppy still looking for a home."

A little silence. Katie had just stared down at her paper, her pencil paused in mid-sentence. But her heart had started thumping. She put down her pencil and tiptoed into the kitchen. Dad was frowning, and didn't seem to notice Katie had joined them; he was thinking hard. Grandma was sitting at the table with her cup of tea, and Katie leant up against her. Grandma found her hand and gave it a squeeze. Katie listened, quietly. And then Dad said:

"Well, the thing is: Kath and I have talked this over, because we know how much Katie wants a puppy. But we can't take a dog on, and that's the end of it." He sighed. "It's the expense – the vet's bills, the food, all the little extras that go with having a dog. There's no way we can manage it."

There it was again. The same old answer.

Never mind, Katie had thought sadly. But she hadn't reckoned on Grandma. She had risked a peep up at her – and seen Grandma's eyes twinkling.

"Right, Matt, but what if I pay the vet's bills? After all, that will be the most expensive bit. It'd be a pleasure to help. Of course it'll be hard work, but I think Katie's old enough now. She's really matured in the last few months – and I know she'd take the commitment seriously. Wouldn't you, Katie?"

Katie nodded. She couldn't even speak.

"Can we at least think about it?" said Grandma.

"Well…" her Dad said cautiously. "All right. Maybe…but that's not a yes," he warned, "it's a maybe."

"And actually Matt," said Mum, turning around suddenly, her hands still covered in flour, "didn't a certain person spend years begging *his* mum for a dog?"

"Yes, he did," chuckled Grandma.

"I had to give in eventually, just to get a bit of peace!"

That was too much for Katie. She flung her arms around her grandmother's neck. "Thank you, Grandma," she whispered fiercely. "Thank you."

Not very long after that, Grandma, Katie, Mum and Dad had gone to see the last Labrador puppy. They had found a tiny scrap of golden fur with outsized paws and enormous floppy ears. He was sitting forlornly in a very big basket, and looked solemnly up at Katie. His little brow was furrowed, his anxious brown eyes soft as melting chocolate. Katie had wanted desperately to touch him – she looked round at Grandma, who was beaming at her.

"Go ahead, say hello," Grandma had said. "But ask him first – let him hear your voice."

Katie had stretched her hand in to reach him, and the puppy had sniffed her fingers shyly.

"It's you," said Katie softly.

His tail had wagged at the sound of her voice.

Can I be yours? he seemed to say. And from that moment he was – he knew it, and even Dad knew it, straightaway.

☆ ★ ★ ❋

Milo had been a little sad that he couldn't go with Katie and Dad to collect the tree. Still, he soon cheered up when he saw it. It was big and rustly and smelt enticingly of outside. Katie had explained about decorating it too, and Milo couldn't wait to get started. He sat on Katie's lap, quivering with anticipation.

But for some reason, Mum didn't want Milo helping at all.

"Mum, please…" Katie protested. "He won't make a mess, I promise!"

But Mum was adamant. "No, Katie. What if he chews on the wire for the Christmas lights? He could pull the whole tree over...he could really hurt himself. Not to mention burn the house down!"

So while everybody else decorated the tree, Milo was shut in the kitchen. He sat under the table and drooped. Mum gave him a special biscuit, and he crunched on it to show her there were no hard feelings, but he still felt very hurt. Why wouldn't Mum let him join in the new Christmas tree game? It was perfect for puppies.

He wanted to help with the lovely crinkly paper chains, and the tinkly, dangly things. Did it have something to do with Katie's new ballet pumps? He had only sucked on the toe a little bit, and Katie had told him she really didn't mind – she could still wear them.

Poor Milo. Like most puppies he had trouble working out what he was and was not allowed to chew. He just could not understand that shoes were not lovely, smelly, munchy toys. He liked to sniff around in the shoe rack in the hall, bottom poking out, little tail wagging. Sometimes he would back out again with a shoe in his mouth, and look imploringly at Katie.

"No, Milo!" she would say gently, trying to ignore his woeful expression.

The final straw for both Milo and Mum had been when he had borrowed one of Grandma's walking shoes from the hall when she was over for tea – and spent a delicious half-hour under the table, quietly destroying it. Luckily Grandma had forgiven him. But Mum had been very cross, and she had moved the shoe rack into the downstairs cupboard.

Katie carried Milo in for one last look at the beautiful Christmas tree, and the little pile of presents underneath it. She held him up to the branches, and let him sniff the spiky pine needles.

Christmas smells good, thought
Milo. He wagged his tail sleepily. And
then Katie took him into the kitchen
to get his basket ready. The little puppy
waited patiently while she shook out and
folded his blanket. Then he climbed in
and curled up, giving a giant yawn. It had
been a long day and Katie was ready for
bed too.

She checked the date on the window
of her advent calendar: 20th December.
Only five days to go! She kissed Milo,
and the puppy gave a little goodnight
sigh; he was almost asleep already. Once
she had filled up his water bowl, and put
down a few extra biscuits – in case he
felt peckish in the night – Katie switched
off the kitchen light and headed up
the stairs.

Chapter Two

The last few days before Christmas were always exciting, but this year was extra special, because Milo was there. And he liked to join in with *everything*.

Mum sat at the kitchen table, pinning the latest Christmas cards onto long red ribbons. Katie was helping cut the lengths of ribbon, and Milo sat on her lap, watching closely, head tilted on one side.

Katie gave him his own ribbon to chew on, so he felt as though he was helping, too.

But Milo was still a very young puppy, and he couldn't concentrate on one thing for very long. From Katie's lap, he could see through his dog flap into the garden. Something swaying up on the fence caught his eye, and Katie felt him suddenly stiffen. What had he seen? Before she had a chance to ask him, Milo scrambled to get down, raced across the kitchen and threw himself through the dog flap, barking at the top of his voice.

Katie stood up and looked through the window, just in time to see Suki, the Siamese cat from next door, leap a foot into the air, lose her balance, and fall off the fence. Milo bounced up to the startled cat. Katie couldn't help giggling. He was so sweet! He was all ears and big paws, and his little tail waved hello, happily.

Will you play with me, Suki?

But Suki was not at all amused. Katie rushed out to pick Milo up, but before she got there, Suki drew herself up, spat crossly, and smacked Milo on the nose.

That would teach him to think twice before ambushing a cat, minding her own business on a peaceful stroll along the fence!

She stalked off, her tail stiff with fury. And Milo went howling back to Katie, his ears drooping and his tail between his legs.

Poor Milo. He stayed close to Katie for the rest of the morning. But after a tender kiss and a long cuddle, he soon forgot about his sore nose, especially because Mum and Katie were making Christmas cake next – and he was allowed to lick the bowl.

Christmas tastes good, thought Milo. He was so small, and the mixing bowl so big, that he climbed into it to finish off, making everybody laugh.

☆ ★ ☆ ✳

Normally Katie found the build-up to Christmas unbearably slow, but time seemed to gallop along with Milo around. She was too busy enjoying her little puppy.

Now, she sat at the table, wrapping presents for her cousins. For once Milo was not on her lap. He was under the table, playing with a scrap of crinkly wrapping paper, rolling and snapping, making tiny little growls.

There was a gentle *thonk* in the hall. Milo immediately flipped over from his back onto his front, and erupted with frantic barking.

Dad leapt to his feet, grinning. "It's the post! Come on, boy!"

The puppy scampered to the kitchen door but Dad made it there first, and stopped, one hand on the door handle. Milo's tail wagged happily. He loved this game.

"Sit…" said Dad. Milo sat back on his bottom, and Dad slowly opened the door. "Go!"

Milo shot into the hallway and skidded to a halt, scattering the pile of Christmas post.

Dad was training Milo, and it was going very well. The only problem was that once he had picked something up in his mouth, Milo was very reluctant to let it go. So every morning, after the race-for-the-post game, Dad and Milo had a tug-of-war as the little puppy hung on determinedly, and Dad muttered firmly, "Drop it…drop it, Milo! Come on, Milo, drop it!"

Eventually Milo would give up the soggy letters, and then Dad would make a huge fuss of him. Although he pretended not to, Katie knew Dad enjoyed this morning ritual as much as her puppy did.

Dad came back into the kitchen, with the ever-so-slightly-chewed Christmas cards and letters under one arm and Milo trotting happily at his heels.

"What a good boy!" beamed Dad,

rummaging in the cupboard for Milo's treat.

Milo sat up proudly, his tail sweeping the floor. He took his biscuit delicately from Dad's hand, and retired to his basket under the kitchen table to crunch on it.

☆ ⋆ ⋆ ✳

Before Katie knew it, she was opening the last-but-one flap on her advent calendar: 23rd December. This was the day that Grandma always visited with presents for everyone. There they were, in a little pile, waiting to go under the tree. There was even a curiously shaped present for Milo. He thought it smelt very interesting, and he longed to open it, but Grandma distracted him with something else – something very special.

"An early Christmas present for you

Milo, for being such a good little puppy. It's a chewy present," she said, as she put the special thing on the floor, next to the squirming puppy. "Because I *do* know how much you love chewing things." And she smiled at Katie.

"Yes, um, we're still sorry about that, Grandma," said Katie, sheepishly. She still felt very bad about not noticing what Milo was up to the day he had wrecked Grandma's shoe. "I just didn't know how much looking after puppies needed," she explained, very seriously.

But Grandma was only teasing. Katie perched on her knee, so the two of them could watch Milo attack his chewy present.

What is it? The thing was huge, almost as big as Milo, with a rich, salty aroma.

"Oh, Milo!" beamed Katie. "You lucky thing! Your first proper bone!"

She watched her puppy circle the bone, examining it from all angles. He managed, somehow, to get his mouth around part of it, and drag it over to his basket. He nudged it up over the side and clambered in.

How clever he was, thought Katie, proudly. He knew just what to do! He turned his little body around in a complete circle twice, to find the perfect position. Then he settled down, with little snuffles and grunts, to a contented afternoon of chewing.

"So," Grandma asked, "are we all set for tomorrow? Presents wrapped?"

But Dad was busy looking for his torch in the cupboard under the sink. "I'm just going check the tyre pressures."

Katie sighed sadly. Every year, on Christmas Eve, her family went to visit her cousins. It was something they always did and normally she looked forward to it. But her little cousins were allergic to dogs – which meant that Milo would have to stay behind. She looked across at him.

The little puppy was curled up in his basket, tired out after all the excitement of his first bone. His tail thumped on his blanket, as he looked back at her, steadily.

"Katie, he'll be fine," said Mum briskly. "It's only a day."

"But, Mum…" Katie hung her head miserably. It was no use – she knew her aunt and uncle wouldn't let a dog in the house, even a tiny puppy. She loved her cousins, but she'd rather not go than leave Milo on his own.

"Come on, Katie," said Dad gently. "Milo will be nice and snug, tucked up in his basket. He'll hardly notice we're gone. You trust me, don't you?"

Katie nodded, blinking back the tears. She went over to sit down next to Milo's

basket, and put her hand on his back.
She was being silly. Milo would be fine
on his own. Wouldn't he?

Chapter Three

The next morning, Mum let Milo out of
the kitchen as she always did. He trotted
to the foot of the stairs, sat down, put his
head back and tried out some of his best
morning barks.

"Sssh! Milo!" called Mum from the
kitchen.

But Katie's bedroom was right at the
top of the house, and she was still asleep.

When she didn't answer, Milo climbed the
stairs. He was still very little, and he had
to jump each step one by one. He trotted
along the landing and then up
Katie's own little attic
stairs – smaller steps
that he could manage
much more easily.
He put up his
paws to push
the door open.
He took a little
run at the
bed – not
that easy, as
there was not
very much
floor space
at all – and

managed to jump and scramble up onto her pillow. He kissed her – a special puppy kiss – and she woke up smiling, as she always did. Milo licked her face again and snuggled down in her arms. Katie stroked her puppy, thinking about the day ahead.

It was Christmas Eve at last. But Katie wasn't as excited as she should have been. It was disappointing to leave Milo now – when they had spent all of the other days together.

☆ ⁎ ⁑ ❇

Katie and Milo had been inseparable since that first day when they had gone to collect him. He had cried all the way back in the car, frightened and lonely in his little box. But when Dad had carried him into the kitchen and put him down gently on the floor, Milo knew who his special person was. He had skittered across the tiles, making straight for Katie.

"Can he sit on my lap?" she had asked Dad breathlessly.

Dad had put the tiny puppy onto her knees. Milo had looked up at her, as if to reassure himself that she was there. Then he had flopped down, and yawned sleepily. He had almost fallen asleep on her knee! His eyes had closed. He had let out a tiny sigh, and one of his big paws had twitched.

"He knows he's home," Mum had smiled.

"Can he sleep on the end of my bed?" Katie had asked, anxiously.

"Well, eventually," Mum had promised. "He does need to be toilet-trained first.

He's only a baby, remember."

Katie, looking down at her sleepy little puppy, had promised herself she would look after him always...

☆ ★ ✸ ✷

Looking down at Milo now, Katie gave a little frown. Today she would have to leave him all alone for hours! He did sleep in the kitchen on his own, so he could manage that. But the rest of the family were usually all ready to come and comfort him if he needed them. Would he be all right, left completely on his own for a whole morning, afternoon and evening?

Milo looked up at her. He could feel how anxious she was. He rolled over onto his back, inviting her to stroke his plump tummy.

"I love you, little Milo," said Katie.
"And I don't want to leave you."

Milo thought he understood what was worrying her. It was true – he didn't much like being on his own downstairs without Katie. He knew he should be sleeping at the end of her bed, so he could guard her properly. On his first night alone, he had whined and scratched at the door, and lain down on the cold stone floor with his nose pressed to the gap, waiting sadly for Katie to come. Sometimes he still felt lonely at night, and he would try barking for her to come and cuddle him.

But he was getting used to it. He liked the noises of night-time – the comforting hum of the fridge, the steady thrum of the occasional passing car. He felt warm and safe in the kitchen, and he loved his chewy toys and his cosy bed. In any case, he was often so tired after a day of discovery that he slept soundly, waking up with a big yawn and a stretch when Mum came in to make breakfast.

He rested his paws on Katie's shoulders and licked her face. *Don't worry,* he tried to tell her. *I'll be fine.*

"Come on, Katie, up you get, love." Mum was calling from downstairs. Katie got dressed, scooped her puppy up, and went down for breakfast.

And then, very soon, before Katie could explain things properly to Milo, Dad had loaded up the car, and it was time to go.

Dad popped his head around the door. "Come on, Katie, stop moping – the sooner we go, the sooner we get back to him." He smiled at her, his eyes crinkling. "And then before you know it, tomorrow will be here and it will be Christmas Day!"

Katie managed a smile at that. She put down some fresh biscuits and water for Milo and kissed him. "See you soon," she whispered.

Milo heard the front door click shut, the car engine purr, and Katie was gone.

Milo was alone. The house felt sad – all ready for Christmas, sparkling with glittery lights and shiny tinsel – but with no Katie calling for him, and no Mum bustling around. He wandered back to his basket, carrying a few biscuits in his mouth. He settled down to gnaw on his snack, and listen for the sound of the car returning. The clock on the wall ticked, and Milo fell asleep.

☆ ★ ✳ ✻

As they drove out of town, the rain drumming on Katie's window turned into sleet. They pulled onto the motorway, and the sleet turned into snow, which blew in gusts at them, forcing Dad to slow down.

"Look, Katie," said Mum from the front. "It's snowing."

"You're not wrong there!" said Dad, humming cheerfully. "I'm...dreaming of a *white* Christmas..." he sang, straightening up in his seat and peering out at the weather. "Yes, this is definitely snow..."

A white Christmas! Katie started to feel a tiny bit excited. She couldn't wait to get back home. Milo had never seen snow!

Milo woke up feeling confused. Was it night-time already? He opened one eye and looked around in the dim light. Something was different, and the little puppy was not quite sure what it was. A strange, muffled quiet had settled over the house, and the air was chilly. He stood up and shook himself awake. He climbed out of his basket and padded stiffly over to the dog flap. A pale light streamed in. Milo put his head to one side, puzzled. What had happened to the world? Where was the grass and where were the trees?

On the other side of the little window, strange, icy white creatures danced in front of his nose. Milo barked at them, but they didn't go away.

☆ ★ ⁂ ❋

Katie looked out of her window. The snow swirled all around the car and she could see it had begun to settle along the grass verges. "Dad!" she said, suddenly. "What if we get stuck? Let's turn around and go home!"

But it was too late to go back. The road in front of them was covered in an icy slurry and all the cars had slowed to a crawl.

"We'll be fine," said Dad. "And we're nearly there. Let's keep going, and see how things are at that end."

Is this a real snowstorm? Katie wondered. *It could be a blizzard!*

"We might be able to go sledging on the hill behind your cousins' house this afternoon, if the snow keeps up," offered Dad, happily.

Katie felt a mixture of emotions. She couldn't wait to try sledging, but what a shame that Milo couldn't be there to join in – he'd love it! She thought of him, chasing after her sledge, flying down the hillside, barking frantically, and smiled to herself. Never mind, she'd tell him all about it just as soon as they got home. And perhaps next year, when he was a little bigger, it would snow again, and he could try pulling her along on a sledge, like a little fluffy snow-dog!

On they drove, slowly and carefully through the swirly snowstorm to her cousins' house.

When Katie's cousins, Jack and Sam, ran out to the car and she saw their excited faces, Katie really was glad she had come, after all.

Once the car was unloaded, Dad turned to the cousins. "What about that old sledge of yours? I've sort of promised Katie," said Dad, and he and her Uncle Robert went off to rattle around in the garage and see what they could find.

An hour later, Katie, her cousins and all the grown-ups climbed up the hillside behind the house with the old sledge from the garage, dusted off and good as new. It had hardly been used, Auntie Claire pointed out – since when had anyone *ever* seen so much snow? The children raced down the slope over and over again, spraying snow everywhere and shrieking with laughter.

Katie hadn't forgotten about Milo, but she *had* stopped worrying. She knew he would wait for her, all cosy and warm, and when she got back, she would sit him on her lap, and tell him all about what it felt like to be out in a snowstorm.

He would listen to her stories, his head cocked, his clever brown eyes watching her gravely, and take it all in. She longed to see him. Perhaps it would still be snowing when they got home, and then she could carry him outside, and they would play in the snow together...

Chapter Four

Feeling confused, Milo stopped barking at the icy shadow creatures and trotted back to his basket. He lay facing the dog flap and dozed anxiously, waiting for Katie to come back.

But Katie didn't come back. As the afternoon wore on, the swirling blizzard outside began to block out the sun. A strange silence settled over the street.

At first Milo kept himself busy watching the twirly white blobs; he didn't take his eyes off them. Every so often, he gave a warning growl from the back of his throat. He would show Katie what a good guard dog he was, and then, maybe, Mum would let him sleep on the end of Katie's bed, so he could look after her properly.

But it was so quiet in the kitchen. Milo could hear his own tummy rumbling. He was all alone, and he was hungry for his supper. He went to his bowl, crunched on a few biscuits and looked up at the kitchen clock. He didn't really understand about time, but he did know it was the clock that told Mum when to feed him. He gave a hopeful little bark. Could the clock please tell him when Katie was coming back?

☆ ⋆ ✶ ❊

After supper, Katie went to the window and looked out. It had snowed so much since they had arrived that she couldn't even make out the shape of their car in the driveway. And it was still snowing! It would be time to leave soon. Katie was missing Milo now, and really looking forward to seeing him.

But Dad came over, and put his hand on her shoulder. "I'm not sure we can drive back tonight, love," he said gently.

Katie gulped. "But Dad! Milo's just a baby – we can't leave him on his own all night!"

Dad didn't reply at first, but then he said, "Milo is a bright little spark. He's got plenty of food and water. He'll be just fine."

Tears rolled down Katie's face.

Jack and Sam pushed out their chairs and came over to look out too. They pressed their faces to the window.

"Wow!" breathed Jack, misting up the glass. "Can we make a snowman? Please, pleeeeaaaase!"

"Good plan, boys," said Uncle Robert. "Maybe we'll make a snow-reindeer instead, for Father Christmas. He'll be coming over the house tonight, won't he, boys? Would he like that, do you think?"

The boys glowed at this idea. They were only five and six, and now they hopped up and down with excitement. "Oh, yes please, Dad! Can we make the antlers too?"

"Wait a minute, I've got another idea," said Auntie Claire. She winked at Katie. "What about making a Mrs Christmas?

Father Christmas would like that better, wouldn't he, Katie?"

All the adults laughed, and the little boys groaned.

But Katie couldn't smile. It was no good Auntie Claire trying to cheer her up. She didn't care what they made out of the snow. She cared about Milo, all alone at home on Christmas Eve.

Chatting happily, the adults and children trooped into the hallway, finding coats and hats, pulling on gloves, but Katie hung back. She wasn't going out to play in the snow.

Milo could be crying for her right now. She wanted to help – and she had an idea.

☆ ★ ☆ ✳

Milo had eaten nearly all his biscuits and

Katie still wasn't back. He was sure now that something was wrong. He didn't want to be a big guard dog anymore. He was only a little puppy, and he missed his Katie. Even the icy shadow creatures had stopped waving at him from outside. The silence felt so lonely, thought Milo, sadly.

A sudden clatter from the worktop in the utility room made him jump. Millie! He wasn't alone after all. Millie had woken up from a long nap and was spinning in her wheel. Milo trotted over to her. With his head cocked in a friendly fashion, he looked hopefully up at her cage. He gave a short bark, like a question mark. His tail swished politely back and forth on the stone floor. *What shall we do?*

But Millie was really quite a simple, silly
creature. She stepped off her wheel for
a moment and looked blankly at him.
Then she went back to her spinning.

Milo padded back to the dog flap and butted his head against it. Dad had locked it – he would never get out this way. Milo gave an anxious little whine, and put his paws up, scratching at the little hatch. It was no use. Even if he could get out, how would he ever find Katie in the new white world outside?

At this thought, Milo gave up trying to be brave, and he howled. *Where are you, Katie?*

But his crying was muffled by the heavy white shroud over the house. Exhausted, he trailed back to his basket.

☆ ★ ✲ ✳

At her cousins' house, while everyone played in the snow, Katie asked Dad if she could borrow his mobile phone. She had decided to call Grandma. If anyone could help Milo, Grandma could. She didn't live that far away from Katie's house, and she was always popping over for tea and crumpets. In fact, Katie remembered that Grandma was out having afternoon tea with the neighbours today. She always went next door for Christmas Eve. All Katie had to do was tell her that Milo was on his own and probably a tiny bit scared and hungry. Even if it *was* too snowy to drive, Grandma would be more than happy to walk over and check on him. Katie was sure her plan would work. She scrolled down to Grandma's name and pressed the little green button. It was ringing.

"Please, please, Grandma. Answer the phone – don't let me down," whispered Katie to herself.

The only flaw in her plan was that Grandma had never really got the hang of her mobile. Half the time she had it on silent, by mistake, and she always looked very surprised when it actually burst into life.

Grandma's mobile rang on and on. She wasn't going to answer it this time. Katie felt hot tears well up in her eyes. Poor Milo. She couldn't help him after all. What was he doing right now, at this very moment?

☆ ★ ✳

In the silent, shadowy kitchen, Milo tried to keep his spirits up. He had a play fight with his ball, rolling over and over with it, growling and snapping. He pulled his blanket out of his basket, and shredded the edges, until his sharp little teeth

ached. He trotted over to his bowl and
drank even more water, which made his
tummy gurgle. He nudged his basket
from one side of the kitchen to the other,
and practised jumping in and out of it.
And then Milo gave up and sat down,
panting, in the middle of the kitchen. He
was beginning to think Katie would never
come back for him. And the house was
getting colder, and darker.

The little puppy was shivering now,
and it was not just the cold that made
him quake. He thought he could hear a
spooky tap-tapping noise. The fur stood
up on the back of his neck, and he gave
a low growl. He crawled back to his
basket, and hid his head under his
blanket. But the noise didn't go away,
and then, just as Milo was plucking up

the courage to look around, he heard
a voice.

Over here, it drawled.

Who was that? Milo lifted his head up.
Is that you, Suki?

At once, the chocolate brown tip of an
elegant tail stopped tapping on the
window.

The Siamese cat gathered herself to sit down primly, and rearranged her tail in a neat coil on the ledge beside her. She stared down at the puppy, her blue eyes glowing like lamps. *Where is Katie?*

In her cage in the utility room, Millie scuttled noisily back to her nest in protest, but Milo didn't care. He desperately needed someone to talk to. Even a not-very-friendly cat like Suki. He scampered over to look up at the window, and put both his paws up on the cupboards. But in one soundless movement, the cat turned and was gone.

Milo gave a little whimper. He trotted over to the dog flap and stared out at the blue-black night. The icy snow flakes had come twirling back, teasing him – but Milo felt too sad to bark at them.

☆ ★ ☆ ✳

Katie's little cousins were sound asleep, tired out after an afternoon of playing in the snow. Katie stood in a pair of borrowed pyjamas. She didn't know it, but she was looking out at the same inky night as Milo. It was snowing again. Tomorrow was Christmas Day and Katie knew she should be excited. But all she could think about was her puppy. What would he do, when he realised she wasn't coming back?

Chapter Five

Milo was only a little dog, but he had a big, brave heart. He wasn't going to give up. He trotted back to his basket and climbed in. He lay down and put his head on his paws. He needed to think.

Milo thought about the first time he had seen Katie. She wasn't shouty and clumsy like other children. She was gentle. She hadn't said very much at first. She had just looked at him with her serious grey eyes. And before she had touched him, she had asked him, "Is it OK? Can I stroke you?"

He had wagged his tail shyly. *Yes.* And she'd tickled him behind the ears, in just the right place. They had shut him in a box to take him away, and he had scratched at it and cried – but all the way back, Katie had leant over the seat and talked to him quietly. The little puppy hadn't understood everything she had said, but her steady voice had comforted him. He knew he was going home.

Katie would never let him down; if she wasn't coming to get him, it was because she *couldn't*. He would have to go to her.

But first he would have to get out of the

house, and now he knew that there was somebody out there who could help him.

In his short life, Milo had already learnt several important things about cats. They were easily offended, and they had very sharp claws. He thought about the last time he had seen Suki – and how sore his nose was afterwards. You had to be extremely polite to cats, thought Milo. They were strange, snooty creatures, but they were clever. And they could get in and out of places. He would talk to Suki, and she would know what to do.

He stood up and gave himself a good shake. *That feels better*. He put his head back and barked for Suki. He yapped, and howled, and growled until his throat ached and his bark was hoarse. And suddenly, the cat leapt out of the black night, and landed silently on the window ledge.

Milo had to talk to her before she disappeared again. He rocketed out of his basket, sending it sliding across the floor, scattering his last few biscuits. He tipped over his water and skidded in the puddle, crashing into the kitchen chairs and knocking one over with a clatter.

But Milo didn't notice – up he jumped, onto the kitchen table. His claws scrabbled on the shiny surface and he almost lost his balance.

He teetered there for a moment, and
then he jumped across to the sink. He
almost fell – but he kicked and scrambled
his way up and over. Dishes and pans
toppled from the draining board. The
washing-up liquid bottle tipped over, and
began oozing onto the floor.

But Milo ignored all this. He put his sticky paws up to the window and waved his tail politely. *Katie's not here. I'm all alone.*

On the other side of the glass, Suki fixed him with an unblinking blue stare. Still looking at him, she washed one paw. It looked as though she wasn't listening. But all the time that Milo was explaining, the tip of her tail flicked back and forth. And then she vanished again.

In what seemed like no time at all, Milo heard a click and the kitchen door swung open. Suki dropped back down on all fours, and stepped in. Milo half-fell, half-scrambled back down to the floor, and trotted over to greet her, but the cat ignored him. She picked her way daintily through the crunchy, sticky mess: past

the upside-down chairs and the slippery
pool of washing-up liquid, drip-dripping
down from the upturned bottle on the
sink. With one flick of a paw, Suki
pushed the catch across. The dog flap
was open. Milo was free!

The little puppy pushed the flap up with
his nose, and sniffed the crisp, cold night
air. He looked back to thank Suki, but he
was not quick enough. The tip of her tail
whipped around the door. She preferred
to leave the house the way she came in,
through the gap in the upstairs bedroom
window.

Milo pushed his head out of the flap
and peered out. A gust of icy wind hit
him, blowing back his ears and making
his eyes water. He hesitated, not sure
what to do next. He did want to go out,

but he didn't like this new white world
very much.

A willowy shadow came towards him through the snowy haze. It was Suki. She beckoned to him with her tail.

That was enough for Milo. He jumped through the dog flap, and landed in the deep bank of soft snow beneath it. He was out!

It was late at night when Katie finally got into the camp-bed in her cousins' bedroom. It didn't feel like Christmas Eve, because her stocking was still at home. With a pang of regret she remembered the special Christmas hat she had bought for Milo. She had so looked forward to her first Christmas with him, and now it was ruined.

Katie sighed. She knew what the funny, heavy feeling in her chest was. It was her heart, aching for Milo. And all the time, there was a lump in her throat that made it hard to swallow, and a weight behind her eyes from trying not to cry.

Even getting into bed reminded her of Milo. She thought of how much he loved her room, and especially her bed. He loved the floaty curtain draped around it,

perfect for wrapping himself in, and for
shredding with his sharp little teeth when
he thought Katie wasn't looking, even
though she was. He loved tramping about
on her puffy duvet, getting tangled in the
folds, his big paws tripping him up. He
should be allowed to sleep on the end of
her bed, Katie thought. She didn't care
what Mum said – he was old enough
now, and they needed to be together.

There was a knock on the door and
Mum came in. She knelt next to the low
bed to kiss her goodnight. "Try and get
to sleep, love." She stroked Katie's hair.
"You really mustn't let yourself worry
about Milo."

"He's still so little, Mum. He'll think
we've left him forever." Katie felt the
tears rising again. But it was no use

crying. There was nothing anybody could do to melt all this snow.

"But at least we know he's safe," said Mum firmly. "He can't get out – that's the main thing. He'll just wait there for us. And we'll be back as soon as we possibly can."

It was easy for Mum to say that, but how could Katie sleep, when her puppy was all alone in an empty house? She lay awake and tried to imagine what he was feeling. He was probably fast asleep, she thought, trying to be positive. She imagined him curled up in his basket, and the thought comforted her. Finally, she drifted off to sleep. But it was a restless kind of sleep, full of strange, shadowy dreams.

Chapter Six

Milo was not *exactly* fast asleep.
Leaving the dog flap swinging, he
walked crunchily out onto the fresh snow,
following Suki's wavy tail. The creamy-
coloured cat sauntered along just ahead
of him, lifting her paws high to clear the
snow. Her four coffee-coloured paws
dipped in and out of the white powder,
leaving tiny, tidy prints. Milo's big paws

scattered the snow everywhere. He kept falling over, sinking down into deep soft drifts. He scrambled up again, shaking off the loose snow, panting, and giving Suki a cheeky doggy grin. Snow was fun! It was cold, but his thick fur kept him warm. He wanted to play!

It was wonderful to be outside after all those hours cooped up in the stuffy kitchen. The snow had stopped falling now. There were fresh drifts on the lawn. Milo scurried back and forth, his nose making trails in the snow. He was trying to pick up familiar smells. Normally he could smell mole, and sometimes fox. He could pick up the nasty smell of rat too, near the garden shed. But now there didn't seem to be any smells at all – they were all hidden underneath this funny, glittery blanket. And the blanket was so soft and billowy! It reminded him of the pillows on Katie's bed. Except those smelt of Katie and these icy clumps smelt of – well, nothing.

He couldn't resist it: he dived head-first into the next pillowy bank, sending a big powdery arc into the air, like a little snowplough. Head up, snorting and blowing snow happily, he spotted another pile, and attacked it with his front paws. He burrowed joyfully down, spraying more snow, until he had made a lovely, deep hole. There was something interesting at the bottom of it too – he rooted it out with his teeth. It was a little clump of snowdrops. He sat back proudly for a moment, panting, and chewing on the little flower. What a shame – it didn't taste very good. It had been a long time since his last biscuit, he thought sadly.

Suddenly Milo heard an impatient *miaow!* Of course – Suki! He spat out his flower and looked around wildly for her. She was right there, sitting like a stone statue on the gatepost, watching him play. Her blue eyes glittered and her whiskers twitched. He wasn't quite sure, but he thought she *might* be smiling.

She jumped down, and led him out of the garden, past a large van parked outside, and rows of cars with snowy roofs. Milo was allowed to trot next to Suki now. She was taking him on her regular prowl around the neighbourhood. He didn't know where he was going, or how they would find Katie. But it was exciting to be out. Where were all the people? Safe and warm inside their houses, thought Milo.

Suki leapt up onto a garden fence and snaked along it, above Milo's head. Her tail was poker-straight now, to help her balance. Milo looked up and saw rows of chimney pots and a starry midnight sky beyond her curved back. The two companions made their way along the road like this – the cat up high, on brick walls and fences, and the little puppy on the snowy paths below. There was a peaceful silence between them.

They came to a dark alleyway between the rows of houses. A bin fell over with a clatter; smelly rubbish tumbled out. An enormous grey rat with matted fur and a horrible, fat tail rushed forward at them, yellow teeth chattering. Milo gave a frightened yelp and shrank back, as Suki drew herself up and spat and hissed. The rat scuttled away, but Suki stayed on the ground with Milo after that.

They walked deeper into the snowy night, turning down a wide, tree-lined avenue. The houses here were much bigger than Katie's, with large bushes and trees in the gardens. A rusty-coloured dog flitted across the road in front of them, and slunk down low, under a car. Milo went bustling over with his tail waving. He pushed his head sideways under the gap. *Hello...I'm Milo.*

Two eyes glowed at him. He heard a snarl, just as his nose sniffed out a wild smell that made him scramble backwards hastily: fox! Suki had retreated to a high wall, and from there, she spat a warning: *Stay back.*

Milo trotted anxiously back across the road and the cat jumped down to reassure him, landing lightly on a high bank of snow by the roadside. She gently butted the trembling puppy with her forehead, and led him away.

It was hours since Milo had last eaten, and the little puppy was very tired. He flopped down in a snowy bank. *Just a little nap...* he thought, sleepily.

Without food to keep him warm, the cold was beginning to seep in under his fur. Would it really matter if he had a little snooze now?

But Suki wouldn't let him rest. She gave him an angry swipe with one sharp claw unsheathed. *Yowl!* Milo felt a stabbing pain on the end of his nose, making his eyes water – but it woke him up just enough to trail after the cat, down a little back street.

They were at the back of a Chinese takeaway. Suki jumped up onto a tall bin to dislodge the lid. Her blue eyes shone. With a practised paw, she

scooped half-full boxes of noodles out
onto the ground next to Milo. He wolfed
down the leftovers, chomping and
slurping, red sauce running down his
chin. Suki sat upright, twisting
the noodles around her
paw, and
nibbling prawns.
Then she
licked her
paws
carefully and
wiped her
whiskers
clean. There
wasn't a single
splash on her
creamy front.

Refreshed, Suki

and Milo set off again. The cat stopped at a thick hedge, with a top hat of snow on it. She opened a gate with her paw and took him up to a wide bay window at the front of a house. She jumped up onto the ledge, and Milo stood up on his hind legs. The curtains were open, and a beautiful Christmas tree glittered and shone with dangly decorations. Christmas tree lights blinked on and off, making Milo think of his own tree, back at home. All around the base of the Christmas tree, Milo saw presents of different shapes and sizes. Wrapped in lovely coloured paper, he thought sadly: perfect for the scrunching and shredding games he liked to play with Katie. He could see a row of stockings hanging up, just like his and Katie's. Then a little girl came in, dressed in her pyjamas, all ready for Christmas morning. She was about the same age as Katie, noticed Milo, and his heart gave a lurch.

Milo turned to look at Suki, sitting neatly on the narrow ledge. Her front paws were tucked under her, and she had gathered her tail into a coil on her back. She stared intently at the family inside. But all the time her long whiskers were reading the night air for danger signals. She kept

the smoky tips of her ears swivelled back,
listening out for trouble.

Life on the streets would
be so scary, thought
Milo. You could never
relax. You'd always
be cold, and hungry.
There would
be nowhere
comfortable and
safe to sleep
either, he
reminded himself
– not like his
snuggly basket.
Milo dropped back
down to the ground. He
had his own little girl, and he missed her.
Where was Katie now? He had a strong

feeling that she was thinking about him. The little puppy felt the fur on his back prickle as he had a sudden, horrible thought. What if Katie came back to the house to find him, and he wasn't there?

Milo wasn't going to find Katie out here. He decided to go home and wait for her. If he went back to the house, she'd come eventually, wouldn't she?

He'd just have to wait as long as
it took. He barked a question at Suki.
Could she show him the way home? The
cat yawned lazily, stretched her back, and
jumped down. That would be no trouble.
It would be dawn soon – she was nearly
at the end of her night-time stalk.

Chapter Seven

Very early on Christmas morning, when it was still dark outside, Katie's little cousins bounced on her until she woke up. They went to fetch their bulging stockings and brought them into her bed.

"You can share, Katie," said Jack.

"But don't eat all the sweets," added Sam cautiously.

Both boys knew Katie's Christmas

stocking and presents were back at her house. They knew this wasn't going to be a proper Christmas for her – and they were trying to help. She smiled at them; they were so sweet.

Dad burst into the room. "Happy Christmas, Katie. And I've got an extra-special present for you." He gave her a big bear hug. "It's stopped snowing, and some of the roads are open."

Katie jumped up, whooping. "Dad! No way! So can we go home?"

Dad gave a cautious nod. "Probably. Let's see how we go."

She threw her arms around his neck, and he held her tightly. Her dad had known how much this meant to her, and he was worried about Milo, too. "But only if you come down and help open some of Uncle Robert and Auntie Claire's presents," Dad smiled down at her. "Got to get some practice in for later on, haven't we?"

Katie couldn't help it. The corners of her mouth twitched and she grinned broadly.

"That's more like it." Dad rumpled her hair. He put his arm around her and they went downstairs to start Christmas with the cousins.

Christmas part one thought Katie. She couldn't wait for part two, with Milo. *Is he awake yet?* she wondered.

☆ ＊ ☆ ＊

Milo was awake, of course, but only just. The little puppy was trudging home in the early morning, trailing behind Suki.

107

It was still dark as they rounded the corner at the top of their street, with Milo's head hanging wearily, his paws dragging in the snow. He looked up and he saw a light coming from his house...Katie was back! He felt a rush of love and a burst of energy. He tore down the street. Suki bounded silently along next to him.

The van they had seen earlier was parked across the driveway. Suki slowed to a walk, and stared at it thoughtfully. But Milo galloped past it. He couldn't wait to see Katie, and tell her all about his adventures. He swerved into the back garden through the gate in a flurry of snow, and dived through the dog flap, making it swing back and forth wildly. With a frenzy of barking, he rushed

through the kitchen, almost losing his
footing on the biscuits he had spilt earlier,
and skidded to a halt in the living room.
He landed on his bottom, rucking up the
carpet, panting happily.

But it wasn't Katie he saw there. A
startled man stood up, with piles of
presents in his arms. He was skinny and
dressed all in black. Behind him in the
hallway, the front door was wide open.
He started to back away from Milo.

It's Father Christmas! thought Milo.
Katie had told him all about the nice man
who came down the chimney into
people's houses to give them presents.
Milo was overjoyed to see him. *Where
are the reindeer?* He was so delighted,
he forgot that Father Christmas usually
wears red, and has a big white beard and
a happy smile, and he forgot all about
Katie for a moment. He threw himself at
the man, whining and barking as loudly
as he could, his tail wagging.

"It's all right, Jake, just a puppy," called

the man over his shoulder to another man who was waiting with the van. "Now then, boy, calm down," he added, looking relieved.

But then a howling, furry streak launched itself into the air from behind Milo. It was Suki! She landed on the man's head, her tail lashing angrily, clawing and hissing.

"Get it off! Get it off me!" he screamed, dropping the presents, clawing at the spitting animal on his head and staggering backwards.

Milo was astonished: what was Suki doing?

But before he could ask her, the man backed into the Christmas tree, knocking it over. It fell to the ground with a crash, and the lights flickered and went out.

The man blindly grabbed hold of the
curtain to keep his balance and pulled it
down. Roaring and waving his arms, he
lurched towards the kitchen.

Milo followed, barking furiously, tremendously excited. He was not really sure why Suki was attacking Father Christmas, but he wasn't going to miss what happened next.

The man had wrenched Suki off his head and he bolted into the kitchen, followed by the determined cat, who called a warning to Milo over her shoulder: *Burglar!*

The floor was covered in soggy biscuits and gooey washing-up liquid. The man skated about wildly on the mess for a few seconds, trying to say upright. He skidded into the utility room and his windmill arms knocked Millie's cage off the side. The cage door swung open and the surprised hamster was catapulted, in her spinning

wheel, out and onto the floor…

The burglar gave a howl of despair. He tripped over the hamster wheel, crashed to the ground and banged his head. With a groan, he fainted.

Suki and Milo looked at each other for a moment across his slumped body. Suki stepped over the burglar and picked her way through the mess. She was headed for the upstairs bedroom window. Her tail brushed Milo's face as she passed him, and he gave her a doggy grin. *Thank you.*

Milo went over and licked the dazed burglar's face. He felt rather sorry for him. Even if he was a burglar, he wasn't a very good one, thought the little puppy. And anyway, he asked himself thoughtfully, what did you do with a burglar if you caught one?

☆ ★ ★ ❋

Katie sat in the back of the car, straining forward as if she could make it go faster just by *willing* it to happen. Every traffic light felt like torture, because it slowed them down. The snow was still piled high in drifts, and the road was icy. Dad had to be very careful, but at least they were on their way. They'd be home soon.

Katie was out of the car first, and ran towards the front door, calling, "Milo! Milo!"

There was no reply.

What's wrong? thought Katie. *Why isn't Milo answering? He* always *barks when he hears us coming back – always, always.*

The door swung wide on its hinges as Katie touched it. Dad came up the path behind her. "Hang on." He put his hand on her arm. "Someone's been at this door. No, don't go in there, Katie!"

"Don't, Katie!" called her mum, running up behind them.

But in a flash, Katie twisted out of Dad's grasp and ran into the hall, calling for her puppy.

She didn't get as far as the kitchen. Milo staggered out sleepily from under the toppled Christmas tree, and caught sight of her. He hurled himself at her, barking frantically, and she knelt down to take him in her arms. He knocked her backwards, and she sat on the ground, hugging and kissing him while he licked her face, and yelped and barked, and wagged his tail, and licked her face all over again. Katie was home. And Milo would never let her out of his sight again.

There was a loud groan from the kitchen. Katie, Mum and Dad looked at each other.

"Be careful, Matt!" said Mum, as Dad tiptoed over to push the kitchen door open wide.

"Ahem," said Dad, as they all stared at the dazed man, slumped on the soggy, sticky floor of the utility room. "Interesting. I think our puppy may have been guarding the house while we were away."

"*Woof!*" said Milo happily. *It was nothing.*

☆ ★ ✳ ✳

Christmas part two didn't take long to organise. Mum called the police, and the burglar was led away, sobbing like a baby, and telling everyone who would listen that he had been attacked by a crazed cat.

"Might have to recommend the pup for a canine medal," said the policeman, kindly. But Milo hid under the table. He didn't want a medal, since Suki really had really been the one who had caught the burglar, and how could he explain that to Katie?

Then Grandma came over and helped Mum clear up the kitchen. And Katie and Milo helped Dad put the Christmas tree upright, and they pinned the torn curtain up. And then Mum put the turkey on, and at last, it was time to open a few presents.

Just as Katie had known he would, Milo loved shredding the wrapping paper, almost as much as the present inside –

a beautiful new collar.

And Grandma gave Milo his curiously shaped, smelly present – the other walking shoe! "Since you chewed the first one so beautifully," she said.

Everyone laughed, and Milo looked very pleased, although he didn't quite understand the joke.

★ ★ ★ ✳

Later that night, Katie lay in bed, looking
up at the zigzag rooftops and the starry
night. She saw a dark silhouette with a
twitchy tail flit across the inky sky: Suki,
out on her midnight prowl, weaving
between the chimney pots, high above
the silent street below.

A few gentle snowflakes were still
drifting down, but the blizzard was over.
Katie looked down at the best Christmas
present of all – Milo the guard dog, curled
up on her feet at the end of her bed.

"Happy Christmas, Milo," Katie
whispered sleepily. And they both fell
fast asleep.

If you liked this book then don't miss...

Beryl
Goes
Wild

by Jane Simmons

Turn the page to read an extract!

When Beryl escapes from the lorry taking her to
the abattoir, she finds a new and frightening world.
A world of wild pigs, where she makes a friend
called Amber, meets the Sisterhood of the Mystic
Boar and goes on an epic journey – but will
she find a home?

A twig cracked nearby.

"Are you all right?" said a small voice.

Beryl looked around. She couldn't see anyone.

Out of the foliage stepped a scruffy little animal.
Beryl blinked at it, trying to work out what it was.
The creature was very muddy, with a pointed snout
at one end and a curly tail at the other. Under all
the brown, straw-like hair and caked-on mud, it

looked like a kind of pig.

Beryl's heart thumped hard against her ribcage as she realised what this strange creature must be.

A wild pig!

"Don't eat me!" Beryl cried.

"Why ever would I eat you?" asked the wild pig. "I saw you fall from the lorry. My name's Amber."

"I'm lost!" squeaked Beryl, as Amber came nearer. Beryl towered above her. She hadn't imagined that wild pigs would be so little. Beryl stretched her whole body upwards, to show Amber how much larger she really was.

"You can come home with me if you want. My Uncle Bert will know what to do," said Amber.

Beryl snorted. She didn't like that idea at all. If Gruff was right, she could catch something nasty from the wild pigs, or even end up as dinner.

What if that creature with the incredibly long ears came back and attacked her? Then her tummy rumbled – she was starving! She felt maybe she had no choice but to go home with Amber.

"OK," she said, and smiled nervously at her.

Beryl followed the wild pig, keeping her distance so it would be hard for Amber to try any funny business. As she stumbled along the track she kept stopping and looking around. She had seen a bit of the outside through the cracks in her sty, but actually being out in it was very strange...

Orchard Books are available from all good bookshops, or can be ordered from our website: www.orchardbooks.co.uk, or telephone 01235 827 702, or fax 01235 827 703.